Two Greedy Bears

Adapted from a Hungarian Folk Tale

By Mirra Ginsburg

Pictures by
Jose Aruego & Ariane Dewey

ALADDIN BOOKS
Macmillan Publishing Company   New York

Aladdin Books
Macmillan Publishing Company
866 Third Avenue, New York, NY 10022
Collier Macmillan Canada, Inc.
First Aladdin Books edition 1990
Printed in the United States of America
A hardcover edition of *Two Greedy Bears* is available from
Macmillan Publishing Company.

10   9   8   7   6   5   4   3   2   1

LIBRARY OF CONGRESS CATALOGING IN PUBLICATION DATA
Ginsburg, Mirra.
 Two greedy bears.

SUMMARY: A clever fox teaches two bears a lesson about greed.
 [1. Folklore — Hungary]   I. Aruego, Jose.
II. Dewey, Ariane.   III. Title
PZ8.1.G455Tw3   [398.2][E]   76 — 8819

ISBN 0-689-71392-4

To Carolyn

Two bear cubs went out to see the world.

They walked and walked, till they came to a brook.

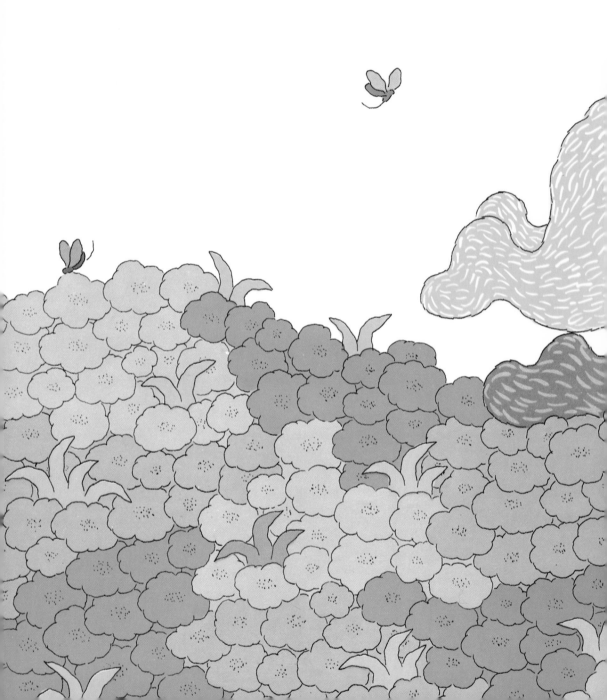

"I'm thirsty," said one.
"I'm thirstier," said the other.

They put their heads down to the water and drank.

"You had more," cried one, and drank some more.
"Now you had more," cried the other, and drank some more.

And so they drank and drank, and their stomachs got bigger and bigger, till a frog peeked out of the water and laughed.

"Look at those pot-bellied bear cubs! If they drink any more they'll burst!"

The bear cubs sat down on the grass
and looked at their stomachs.

"I have a stomach ache," one cried.
"I have a bigger one," cried the other.
They cried and cried, till they fell asleep.

In the morning they woke up feeling better
and continued their journey.

"I am hungry," said one.
"I am hungrier," said the other.

And suddenly they saw a big round cheese
lying by the roadside. They wanted to divide it.
But they did not know how to break it into equal parts.
Each was afraid the other would get the bigger piece.

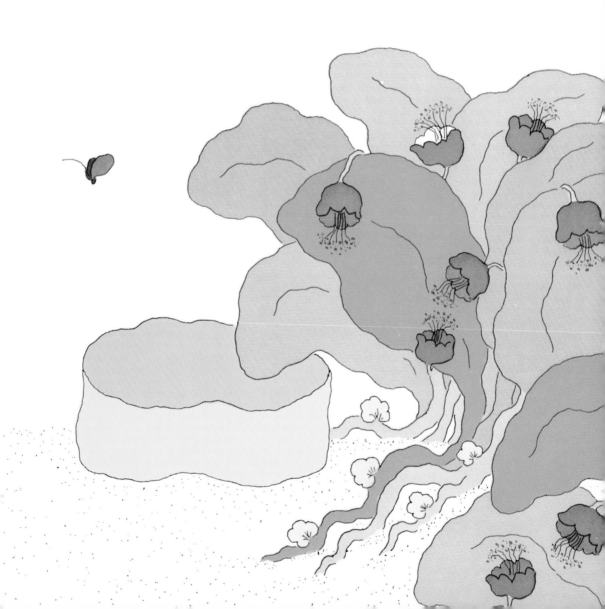

They argued, and they growled, and they
began to fight, till a fox came by.

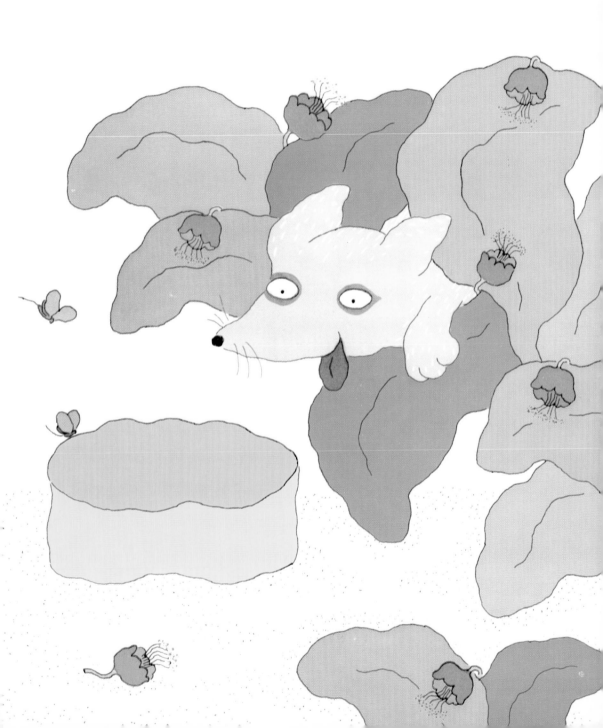

"What are you arguing about?" the sly one asked the bear cubs.
"We don't know how to divide the cheese so that we'll both get equal parts."
"That's easy," she said. "I'll help you."

She took the cheese and broke it in two.
But she made sure that one piece was bigger
than the other, and the bear cubs cried,
"That one is bigger!"

"Don't worry. I know what to do." And she
took a big bite out of the larger piece.
"Now that one's bigger!"

"Have patience!" And she
took a bite out of the second piece.
"Now this one's bigger!"

"Wait, wait," the fox said with her mouth full of cheese. "In just a moment they'll be equal."
She took another bite, and then another.

And the bear cubs kept turning their black noses
from the bigger piece to the smaller one,
from the smaller one to the bigger one.
"Now this one's bigger!"
"Now that one's bigger!"

And the fox kept on dividing and dividing
the cheese, till she could eat no more.
"And now, good appetite to you, my friends!"
She flicked her tail and stalked away.

By then all that was left of the big round
cheese were two tiny crumbs.
But they were equal!